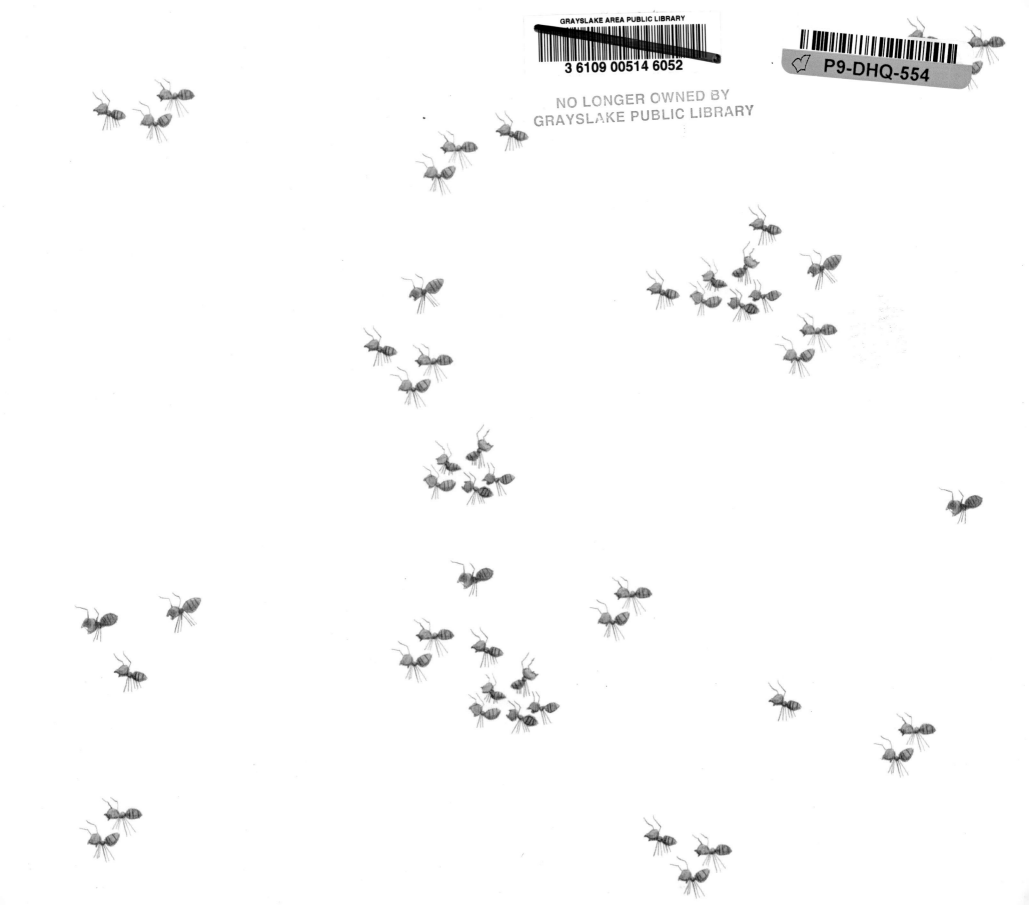

GRAYSLAKE AREA PUBLIC LIBRARY

3 6109 00514 6052

NO LONGER OWNED BY
GRAYSLAKE PUBLIC LIBRARY

P9-DHQ-554

E
AMAVISCA,
L.
1.17 dz

To Lola, who was on her way.
To Nicolas and Carlos.
To you.
Luis Amavisca

To Pablo and to my parents,
for always being by my side.
Esther G. Madrid

Bang Bang I Hurt the Moon
Somos8 Series

© Text: Luis Amavisca, 2015
© Ilustrations: Esther G. Madrid, 2016
© Edition: NubeOcho, 2016
www.nubeocho.com – info@nubeocho.com

English translation: Luis Amavisca & Martin Hyams
Text editing: Caroline Dookie

Distributed in the United States by
Consortium Book Sales & Distribution

First edition: 2016
ISBN: 978-84-944446-7-8
Printed in China

All rights reserved.

3 6109 00514 6052

BANG BANG
BANG
I HURT THE
MOON

Luis Amavisca

Esther G. Madrid

nubeOCHO

GRAYSLAKE AREA PUBLIC LIBRARY
100 Library Lane
Grayslake, IL 60030

Through the window,
the light of the full moon came in.

Mom had read a bedtime story.
She gave them a goodnight kiss.

Nicholas was not sleepy.

He started kicking under the sheets, playing with his hands and making the shape of a gun.

He pointed at Charlie and whispered,
"Bang Bang!"
His elder brother said, "You know Mom
doesn't like these games."

Nicholas looked through the window
and made a naughty face...

He pointed his hands at the moon.
"Bang Bang! I shot the moon!"
His brother shouted, "Look!"

Something incredible was happening.
The moon started to fall from the sky!

They quickly left their bedroom.
Mom was frightened. She was looking out the window.

Together they ran out of the house...
There it was, the moon, in their garden. A huge, round, fat,
beautiful moon. Its eyes were closed and it shone like silver.

Mom was panicking. Nicholas started crying and hugged his mother's leg. "It was me, it was me! I killed the moon!"

Just at that moment, the moon opened its eyes,
"I'm not dead! I've just fallen from the sky. It was a tremendous fright.
The problem is that now I don't know how to get back up."

"So how can we help you?" asked Charlie.

They tried to move it, but it was just too, too heavy.
While they were thinking of how to help the moon,
they thought they heard a voice. An ant spoke to them,

"The Great Mountain is very close to the sky, perhaps it would be easier to get the moon back up from there." Charlie replied, "But how will we take the moon there?"

"We could carry it all together."
"You're so tiny, how will you do that?"
asked Nicholas.
"Together we are strong. Let´s go!"

Wasting no time, the ants began
to work. They all got beneath
the moon and started to lift it up.

And they all set off for the Great Mountain,
a line of ants carrying the moon,
a woman and two boys.

It was going to be a long night,
but the moonlight accompanied them.

They walked through a forest and they followed many footpaths.
Nicholas was tired. "Climb on top of me" said the moon.
"Aren't you upset?" asked Nicholas.

They finally reached the mountaintop.

"Will you now jump to get back up?" asked Nicholas.
The moon smiled. "I can't jump, I don't have legs like you."

In the distance they heard birds singing.
It was nearly morning.

A small sparrow came very close.
"What is the moon doing down here?
Dawn is breaking and it needs to go to sleep!"

Charlie told the bird what had happened.
Then, after thinking for a few seconds,
the sparrow said, "My friends and I will
help the moon get back up."
"You're so small, how will you do that?"
asked Nicholas.
"Together we are strong."

The sparrow began to whistle and within seconds,
dozens of birds arrived.

A golden light started to appear on the horizon. Very soon
the sun would rise and they didn't have much time.

More and more birds came to help, some carrying string in their beaks.

With incredible skill,
the birds tied a huge circle of string
to the moon and from each string,
hundreds of birds began to pull.

The moon began to rise above the ground. Its silver light shone from above. On the horizon, the golden sun began to appear.

"Hurry up! We don't have much time!" urged the sparrow.

When the birds were high enough, they all
released their strings at the same time.
Amazingly, the moon was back in the sky again.

The moon smiled and said goodbye to the family,
the ants and the birds, "Thank you."

A few minutes passed, the sun peeked over the horizon.
And the moon slowly started going down the other side.

The family would never forget that night.

And so it was that Nicholas never again played with guns...
Because it might hurt the moon.

GRAYSLAKE AREA PUBLIC LIBRARY
100 Library Lane
Grayslake, IL 60030

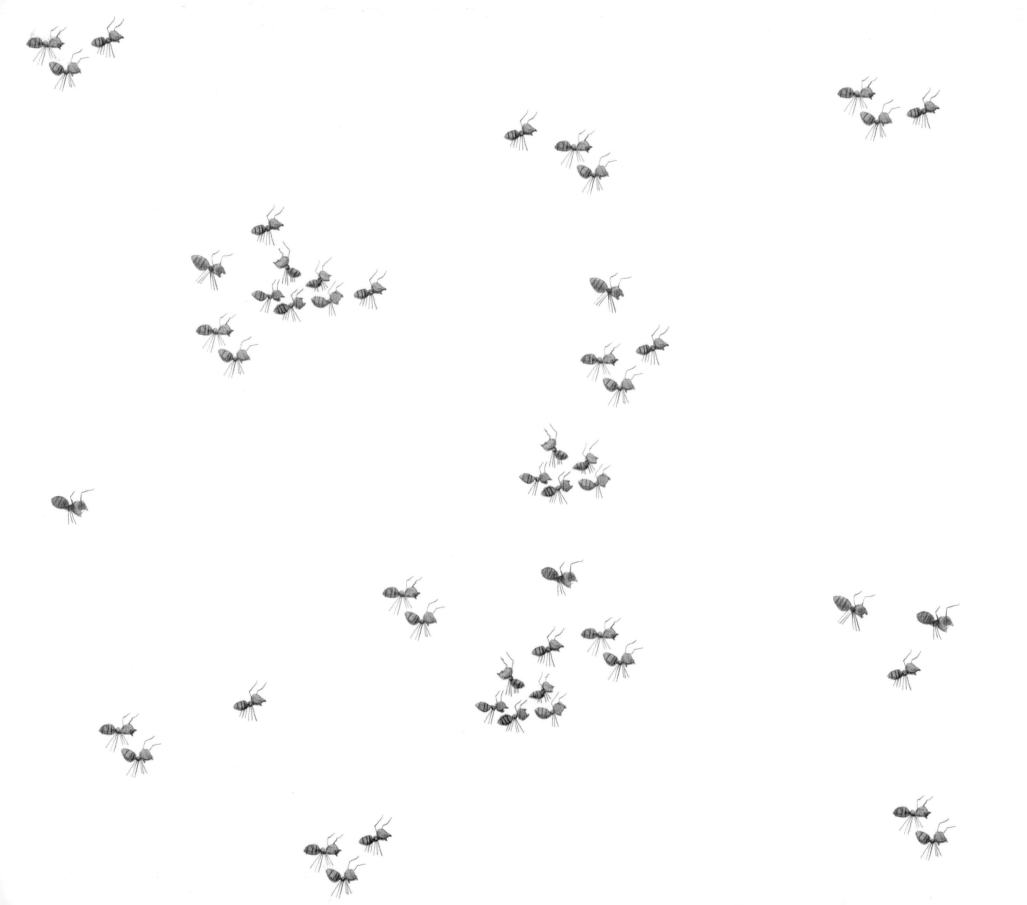